Items should be returned on or b
shown below. Items not already r
borrowers may be renewed in pe
telephone. To renew, please quot
barcode label. To renew online a PIN is required.
This can be requested at your local library.
Renew online @ **www.dublincitypubliclibraries.ie**
Fines charged for overdue items will include postage
incurred in recovery. Damage to or loss of items will
be charged to the borrower.

Leabharlanna Poiblí Chathair Bhaile Átha Cliath
Dublin City Public Libraries

Baile Átha Cliath
Dublin City

Leabharlann Shráid Chaoimhín
Kevin Street Library
Tel: 01 222 8488

Date Due	Date Due	Date Due

For my nephew, Frank Johnson,
as promised – Alan Durant

For Jacks (and Marly) who helped me on to the
first rung of the ladder. X
And for Alsie Durant – thank you. X
Sue Mason

First published in 2006 in Great Britain by
Barrington Stoke Ltd
18 Walker Street, Edinburgh, EH3 7LP

www.barringtonstoke.co.uk

This edition first published in 2011
Reprinted 2014

4u2read edition based on *Game Boy*, published by
Barrington Stoke in 2003

A CIP catalogue record for this book is available
from the British Library upon request

ISBN: 978-1-84299-912-7

Printed in China by Leo

Contents

Level 1

John Paul held his left thumb down on the controls of his GameBoy. His other thumb was over the A button. He had to get the timing just right or he'd end up in a pit of filthy slime.

NOW!

His right thumb jabbed down on the A button. On screen, Space Man jumped and ...

made it! His hands grabbed the edge of the rock. His body and legs swung in the air.

But he was not out of danger yet. An alien was marching up and down on the rock above him.

The alien had a splat gun. One blast from that gun and that was the end of Space Man.

JP had to get the timing and speed just right again. As soon as the alien turned his back Space Man stood up. A quick jab on button B and he had a flame thrower in his hand. The alien turned round. John Paul fired three times. Flames shot out. The alien fell with a cry. A moment later, he'd melted.

JP grinned. He loved zapping aliens. In fact he loved zapping anything – aliens, snakes, dinosaurs, apes, anything. If it moved, he'd zap it!

He pressed down on the controls again and rushed on to the end. There was a blast of loud music. A clock came up on the screen. Its hands spun wildly. Then at last they stopped.

His time flashed up: 2 minutes, 27 seconds! He'd done it! This was 4 seconds less than last time. He didn't know anyone who had done Level 7 of Alien Attack that fast. He was the champ! Someone was coming up the stairs. JP turned off his GameBoy. There was a ping and it went dead.

JP's mum put her head round the door. "You should be reading," she said, "not playing with that thing." She nodded at the GameBoy.

"I wasn't playing with it," JP lied.

"Well, I can't see a book in your hand," his mum went on.

JP gave a yawn. "I'm a bit sleepy now, Mum," he said. "I think I'll read tomorrow."

"Make sure you do," said Mum.

She turned out the light and kissed JP good night.

JP smiled. His mum had gone. "Sorted," he said to himself.

Level 2

John Paul was coming home from school on his bike the next day. The wind was at his back and he was racing down the hill past the shops.

Suddenly a big, black cat ran out from between two parked cars in front of JP. But he didn't slow down. He just yelled at the cat and rang his bell again and again. The cat got out of the way just in time and shot under one of the parked cars.

JP stopped and got off his bike to look at the cat. It was shaking and looked very scared. Its tail was all fluffed up.

"Silly cat," JP told it. "You nearly got zapped."

When JP looked up, he was amazed to see that there was a new shop in the street. It hadn't been there the last time JP had gone past. But it looked very old. Its window was full of junk, a cracked vase, a broken chair, some dusty plates, and some CDs with no boxes to go with them.

Then JP thought he saw something else in the window. He came closer. Yes, he was right. It was a GameBoy game. And even better, it was one he'd never seen before!

JP went into the shop. There was an old man behind the counter. He was almost bald, with just a small tuft of white hair on

top of his head. He looked at JP through thick glasses that made his eyes look huge. They were odd eyes too. They shone in the middle as if they had a light inside them.

JP felt a bit spooked, but he tried not to let the man see. "I'd like to have a look at that GameBoy game in the window," he said. "I've never seen one like it before."

The man's eyes seemed to get even bigger. "That's not a game," he said. "That's for real."

"Oh, right." JP smiled. "What's it called, then?"

"Call it what you want," said the man. "Some call it life, some call it death. It's all up to how good a player you are." He smiled at JP.

This man is weird, thought JP. "What do you mean?" he asked.

"If you buy it, you'll see," said the man. "You do want to buy it, don't you?"

"Too right," said JP. "How much do you want for it?"

They fixed on a price. JP paid and set off again on his bike. He was glad to be out of that shop. That old man had been really spooky.

Level 3

JP went up to his room as soon as he got home. His mum was making tea down in the kitchen, so she wouldn't bother him for a bit.

He looked at the game. It had no picture or name on it. All it had was one line of print. It said: WARNING! THIS GAME MAY BE VERY BAD FOR YOU.

dum
dum
dum
dum
dum
dum
Dum
dum
dum
DUM
dum
dum
dum
dum
dum
DUM
dum
dum
dum
dum
dum
dum

JP shook his head. This was an odd game. He was longing to find out what it was all about.

He got his GameBoy down from the shelf and loaded the game. He flicked the switch and the GameBoy came to life with a ping. Some words flashed on to the screen. They said: WARNING! ONCE YOU START, YOU CANNOT GO BACK!

JP laughed. Were the words trying to put you off playing? He pressed the start switch. Loud, deep music began to play. Dum dum dum dum dum, dum dum! Dum dum dum dum dum, dum dum! This was more like it.

On the screen someone was standing in a hot desert. In front of him was a pile of rocks. JP looked around to see if there was a weapon for him to pick up. Yes, there, shining by a rock – a big dagger. JP pressed the right button and the person ran towards the dagger. He bent down and picked it up.

Good, now he had a weapon. JP hoped that there would be a gun for him to pick up as well – maybe at the next level. Then he could do some real zapping. He pressed the B button to put the dagger away. Then he pressed the controls and the person ran on.

He was in among the pile of rocks now. He ran on. Up and down he went. A tall rock blocked his way. No problem. A flick of the controls and the person bent over and began to roll.

He went into a tunnel and out the other side. Then he was standing in front of a yellow spiky bush. It blocked his way.

JP smiled. These were the moments he loved. He pressed button B and the dagger flashed on the screen. He pressed button A and the dagger cut away at the bush. Whomp, whomp, whomp! He slashed at the bush until it was gone. Then he put the dagger away, grinned and moved on.

He went up over more rocks, jumping and rolling, on and on …

JP had begun to feel that this was all too easy. He'd played much harder games than this. Where were the dangers?

Whoa! JP stopped just in time. Right in front of him, rising from under a rock, was a snake with two heads. It flicked its heads at him and hissed. One more step and he'd have been dead. And he didn't want to go all the way back to the start at this stage.

The snake hissed again. The sun felt very hot. JP's hand felt damp as it closed over the dagger.

Wait a moment. Run that last bit again.

JP's hand felt damp as it closed over the dagger. His hand. He looked down. He looked up. He was standing among the rocks under the bright sun. In front of him was a snake with two heads, hissing at him.

This is like a bad dream! It's not a game at all.

But all this was not on a screen – the snake was really there. And so was JP.

He was in his bedroom playing with his GameBoy wasn't he? No, he wasn't. He was part of the game now. He was playing it from the inside!

JP took a step forward then jumped back as the snake almost got him. The near miss made him think hard. He took a step forward as the snake drew back. Then he lifted the dagger to strike. As the snake's heads flicked again, he moved fast. One slash, two slashes. Whomp, whomp! The heads fell off and the snake was gone.

JP walked on, with great care, under an arch ... and everything went black.

Level 4

A moment later it was light again. The rocks had gone. He was on a large, flat stone at the boggy edge of a river.

"I must have come to the end of that last level," he said to himself. What had his time been? *It must have been good*, he thought.

JP sat on the stone to think. It seemed to him that the game in his GameBoy could somehow make the world on the screen seem real. But how? Was there some secret signal in the screen? Or did it pass into his fingers as they pressed the control buttons? Whatever it was, it was amazing.

So this is why the man in the shop had said the game was for real. But it was a bit over the top to call it life or death. It was still only a game – even if it was a fantastic one.

Well, he was ready for the next level. It was time to move on.

JP looked in front of him. There were lots of paths through the bog. They were marked by logs and stones. There must be hidden dangers out there, so he'd have to take care.

Croak! A noise above him made him jump. A huge bird with a long, sharp beak swooped at him, coming much too close. JP began to run.

He chose a large stone to begin crossing the bog. Then he jumped onto the next one. Then to the side. Then on again – and to the left. So far, so good.

He checked out his next step. He could choose one of three stones or a log. *Not the log*, he thought. It was half under the bog and didn't look very safe. One of the stones had a mass of green moss all over it. He might slip on that. So that was out. That left two stones to choose from, one to the left, one to the right.

The one to the right looked flatter. OK. He took a small step and jumped.

Bump!

Slosh!

Argh!

The stone sank under JP. The bog sucked at his feet. It was as if someone was under there trying to grab him and pull him down.

JP fought hard, trying to drag himself free – but the bog was too strong. It was going to pull him under. He felt a rush of panic. He had to get free!

The bog was up to his knees now and was rising. Only one thing could save him. The log. If he threw himself forward he could just about get his hands on it.

The log didn't look very safe but he had to get to it. The bog tugged at his legs. He fell forward, trying to get hold of the log.

He felt the bark scrape his hands as he grabbed it and tried hard to pull himself up.

It was a life and death battle. At first he thought the bog was winning, but slowly he pulled his body up onto the log. Then his legs. And last of all his feet popped free. JP lay on the log, panting.

After a bit, JP was able to sit up. He was muddy and damp, but he felt fine. The bog hadn't got him, that was the main thing. *I should have picked this log to move to in the first place*, he thought. *I must be more careful next time.*

He got up slowly. He was well past the middle of the bog. There was a line of logs that looked as if they'd take him the rest of the way. But could he trust them?

Well, nothing could be as bad as the sinking stone. And he was still alive. He smiled. What did he have to lose? It was only a game after all.

He jumped onto the next log, walked along it and jumped again. Three logs, four logs ...

He was on a roll. This was pips – easy peasy! There were only two more logs to go and then he'd be on the other side of the bog, another level over. He jogged along the log and was just about to jump, when ...

Hold on!

JP stopped so suddenly that he almost fell forward. There was something odd about the next log. He was sure it had moved. Just a bit, but yes, it had moved.

JP gazed at the log, waiting to see if it moved again. It didn't.

But JP was going to be careful. He didn't want to make another bad mistake like the sinking stone. He bent down and tore a large bit of bark from the log he was standing on. He threw it into the water just in front of the log.

Whoosh!

JP drew back in panic, as a set of huge teeth crushed the bark with one snap. In a second the teeth had gone again.

But JP knew what he'd seen: a wide mouth, strong jaws and dark hooded eyes – the log wasn't a log at all. It was a crocodile!

Now JP had a problem, a big problem. The log he was standing on had begun to sink. And there were only two places he could move to: back to the stone that had sunk under him before or onto the crocodile.

After his moment of panic, JP felt quite cool. He'd faced problems like this lots of times before, playing his GameBoy.

He made up his mind fast. He knew what he had to do. If he jumped and then ran really fast, he could get past the croc and

onto the next log. Then, with one more jump he'd be at the end of the level. And if he got it wrong, well, it was only a game …

He was ready for this now. His heart was pumping. He took two steps back on the sinking log, and then jumped. He raced over the croc's back. He needed to leave his next jump to the last moment if he was going to get safely over the croc's head.

One, two, three, four, five, six, seven …

JP sailed over the croc's head. He felt the snap of jaws at the back of his legs. He ran for his life over the other logs.

He didn't look back. He was over the last log in a flash and onto the large, flat stone that marked the end of the bog. He gave a yell and held up his arms. He'd done it. "Result!" he cried.

Everything went black.

Level 5

Birds sang. A monkey howled. Some way off, a lion roared.

JP looked around him. He was in a jungle – and it was hot. Already his face was damp with the heat. The back of his right leg felt damp too.

He looked down ... and gasped.

His leg was wet with blood! There was a hole in his trousers and a gash on his leg. The croc's teeth must have torn into him as he jumped.

So in this game, there could be real blood. Cool!

The gash wasn't very deep, but it hurt. JP ripped a bit of cloth from his torn trousers and tied it round the gash.

Yes, that felt better. But something wasn't quite right. OK, he'd had this gash from the croc. But that was on the last level. This was a new level and he should be fine again by any normal GameBoy rules. *But then I should know by now*, thought JP, *that this isn't a normal game. It's for real*. And JP wanted more!

JP began to walk into the jungle, taking care to look out for dangers. He brushed away huge leaves and pushed his way past thick bushes. He used his dagger to hack a path when the jungle got too thick.

It was hot work. JP wiped his damp face. Once he nearly fell into a deep pit, but saw it just in time and jumped across. He couldn't see what was down there in the pit, but he could hear lots of hissing. He was sure there were snakes in there. He went on into the jungle. He jumped over another pit full of sharp spikes. Then he grabbed hold of a vine and swung himself over another pit. He was starting to enjoy himself a lot.

Squawk! Squawk!

JP looked up to see a large parrot sitting on the branch of a tree. Then he saw something else – something hanging from the tree. It was purple and shaped like a diamond. It had a stem and seemed to be growing on the tree like some odd sort of

fruit. But what was most odd of all was the fact that it was the only one on the whole tree.

JP had played a lot of games and knew that there was always something to collect as you went through each level. It might be a flag, or a coin, or a medical pack to help you if you got hurt. This fruit must be that sort of thing. Anyway, he wanted to get a closer look.

He looked hard at the tree to see how he could get up into it. The trunk looked too smooth for him to get up that way, but one of the branches hung down quite low. If he jumped up and grabbed it, he might be able to pull himself up. It was worth a try.

He ran forward, jumped and grabbed hold of the branch. For a few seconds he swung in the air, legs flapping, then he pulled himself up and up.

At last he was sitting on a firm branch, with the diamond fruit just above him. Its skin was very smooth and shiny. JP held his hand out to feel it.

Squawk!

JP almost fell off his branch, thinking the parrot was going to peck him. But it didn't. It just sat on its branch glaring at him with its big, beady eyes.

JP grinned. "What's the matter with you, Polly?" he said. "Don't you want me to take your fruit?" He shook his head. "Well, I'm sorry, but that's the game."

He put his hand up again, thinking this time he'd pick the fruit.

Squawk!

JP just smiled. In a moment, he'd have that shiny, purple fruit in his hand. There was nothing the parrot could do to stop him. He just had to stretch a little more …

SQUAWK!

"Yah!" JP's fingers felt something hairy. A sharp pain shot up his arm. There was a large spider on the fruit and it had bitten him. JP was angry with himself. He should have been ready for the danger.

JP's anger soon turned to worry. The spider looked like a tarantula, which meant he was in real danger. Even now his hand was swelling up and going purple from the poison.

He began to feel sick. What had the man in the shop said about the game: "Some call it life, some call it death. It's all up to how good a player you are." Well, JP was good – and now he was going to have to show just how good.

He knew that he had only one chance to save himself: he had to get that fruit. But just how fast could he move?

He reached up with his other hand, making sure it was well away from the spider. He was damp all over now from the heat and the worry and the poison that was creeping round inside his body.

JP waited ... Now! As the spider went round to the other side, JP snatched the fruit and slammed it onto the branch. Half of the fruit was squashed but so was the spider. JP had zapped it!

"Result," he said weakly.

JP took a deep breath, closed his eyes and bit into the purple fruit.

"Ah," he said with a sigh as he felt the sweet fruit soothe and refresh him, getting rid of the poison.

Then he fell out of the tree.

Level 6

JP was in some kind of cave. There were flaming torches on the walls. In front of him the cave split into two tunnels. Which one should he choose: the right or the left? He'd chosen to go right in the bog; so this time he went left.

JP took one of the torches off the wall and walked into the tunnel. He couldn't see very far ahead, so he went slowly. Anything might be waiting for him in the darkness.

JP walked for a long time. But apart from a few cracks in the ground that almost tripped him up, the tunnel had no dangers. But it didn't go anywhere. It came to a dead end.

JP sat down to rest. He was worn out and his bad leg hurt him. For the first time he thought about home and his bed and how nice it would be to get back there. This was a cool game, but how many more levels were there? When would he get to the end?

After a bit JP got up again and walked back along the tunnel into the cave. Now there was only one way to go.

Let's hope this way goes somewhere, he thought. He knew he wasn't going to get the best time for this level. He must have been down here for ages.

JP went a little faster down the right tunnel than he had gone down the left. He didn't like this dark world much and was keen to get out of it. The bog and the jungle had been a lot more fun – even with the croc and the spider. This level was just, well, dull.

Rumble, rumble!

What was that? The ground started to shake under his feet. There was a booming sound in his ears. He walked a little slower, holding the flaming torch well in front of him. The noise got louder and louder. The ground shook more and more. What could it be? JP took out his dagger just in case.

And then he saw it. It was huge: a giant ant-like thing that filled the tunnel from top to bottom, side to side. Each move of its feet shook the ground. It glared down at JP

with huge, red eyes. Then it opened its mouth.

JP cried out and fell back. The giant ant had teeth like knives.

The ground shook again as the thing moved towards JP. His heart was beating like a crazy drum. The dagger slipped from his hand and clinked on the floor. A picture came into his head of that big black cat he'd nearly zapped. Well, now he knew how that cat felt. He was scared out of his wits.

He'd had enough of this game. He didn't want to play any more. He wanted to be back in his room, at home, with his GameBoy. A thought flashed into his mind. Who was at the GameBoy's controls now? But he had other things to worry about. The giant ant was getting closer and closer. Any moment now it was going to zap him! He had to do something fast. Think, JP, think!

JP could just see something behind the huge ant. It was a door. That must be the end of the level! He had to get there. The ant was almost on him.

If I was playing the GameBoy now, what would I do? he asked himself. *I know, I'd roll!*

Quick as a flash, JP got down. Then he rolled for his life. He rolled between the giant ant's tree-like legs and under its huge body – and then he was in front of the door. JP pulled the handle, and the door opened. He went through.

Once again, everything went black.

Level 7

JP looked around him. He was in a large room. It was full of walk-ways on different levels with lots of ladders to climb. It was like a huge game of snakes and ladders – only there were no snakes.

Well, that's what JP hoped anyway. He was fed up with snakes and spiders and giant ants. Still, there would be some sort of danger, he was sure of that.

At the far end of the room, on a high platform, were three large books. There were two huge words written in bright lights above the books. They just said *THE END*.

JP smiled. This was it – he'd got to the last level. Very soon he'd be at the end and then he could get out of this crazy game. He set off, up a nearby ladder.

There were more dangers, but he was ready for them. There weren't any creatures this time, but there were trap doors hidden in the walk-ways. They were hard to spot but JP was very careful. Once he did put his foot on a trap door. But he was able to pull it back in time as the door dropped open. So he didn't fall through. The near miss made him even more careful. It was only 50 metres from the door to the other end of the room and the books, but it took JP ages to get there. He didn't want to make a mess of things now he was so near the end.

JP was in a kind of maze. A lot of the walk-ways were dead ends and again and again he had to turn and try another way. But at last he was at the foot of the tall ladder that would take him up to the platform where the books were. He went up it feeling very excited.

The platform was very small. There was only just room for him and the books. Each book rested on a gold stand. JP stepped onto the platform and a red light flashed above him.

More words came up under where it said *THE END*.

Then the words had gone. In their place was a clock. Its hand started to move round. As JP watched, 10 seconds went by. He had to act fast.

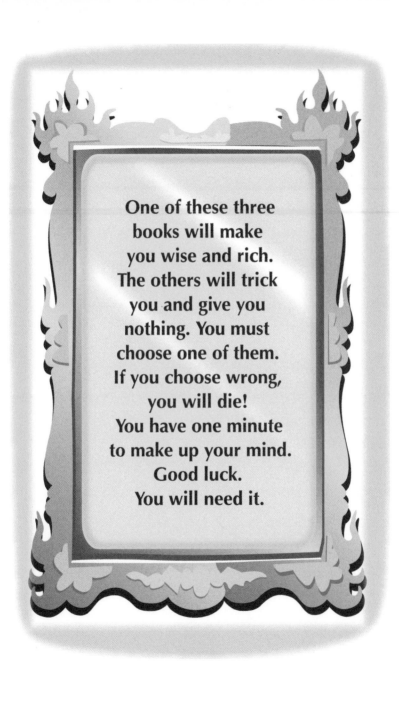

One of these three
books will make
you wise and rich.
The others will trick
you and give you
nothing. You must
choose one of them.
If you choose wrong,
you will die!
You have one minute
to make up your mind.
Good luck.
You will need it.

JP stared at the books, one after another. The first was splendid. Its cover was of gold set with costly jewels. *It must be worth a fortune*, JP thought.

He looked at the second book. It was made of tiger skin with a spine of white ivory. Like the first book, it looked as if it must be worth a lot of money.

JP moved on to the third book. Well, this one didn't look much at all. The cover was plain red cardboard and tatty – it was the kind of book you might find at a car boot sale or in a junk shop. *It can only be worth a few pence*, he thought.

He looked back at the clock. Only 30 seconds left ...

JP looked again at the three books. It had to be the book with all the jewels. Of course that was worth the most money. It was simple! He stepped towards it ... then stopped.

It was too simple. A thought came into his head – something his mum often said: *Never judge a book by its cover.*

40 seconds gone ...

JP's hands were damp. His heart was pumping again.

45 seconds gone ...

Not the book with the jewels then. It must be the second book with the tiger skin. He put one hand out to open it, then stopped again. Tiger skin. Ivory. These came from animals that had been killed for their skins or tusks.

JP liked zapping things in his GameBoy games, but he knew that killing real tigers and elephants was wrong. There were only a few left and they were at risk. How could any book that had tiger skin and ivory make you wise?

50 seconds ...

What should he do? It couldn't be the third book. Surely, not the third book.

52 seconds ...

Look at it. It wasn't worth anything. It was junk.

54 seconds ...

Junk! JP's brain sparked into life.

56 seconds ...

Where did this game come from? It came from a junk shop!

58 seconds ...

But the book was so tatty!

59 seconds …

He had to choose.

This was it then. He was going to die!

JP took a step forward and opened the third book …

The red light flashed again. The clock had gone. Flames shot out of the gold book and the tiger skin book and then they too were gone. The platform slid away.

JP dropped like a stone down into the dark.

Level 8

JP's thumbs were on the control buttons. His eyes were gazing at words on the screen: "Well done! You made it. You're still alive. Do you want to play again?"

"No fear," JP said. He turned off his GameBoy. Then he lay back on his bed and took a deep breath. His heart was pumping and his whole body was shaking. That game had been really scary.

He thought about that last level. He'd chosen the right book, but what if he'd chosen one of the other ones? Would the flames have got him too? He'd be dead now. Really dead. Or had it all been a game? Well, anyway, it had been just too real for him to be much fun. He had no wish ever to play it again. In fact, he was going to take it back to the shop right now.

JP looked at his watch. He must have been away for hours. But he hadn't. He was amazed to see that no time had passed at all. He could hear his mum getting tea ready in the kitchen. JP took the game out of the GameBoy and ran into the hall.

"Mum, I'm just going up to the shops," he called. "I'll be back very soon."

He ran out of the house without waiting for his mum to reply.

He ran all the way to the shops, taking the short cut past the river. There were lots of things he wanted to ask that weird man in the junk shop: How did the game work? Were there others like it? Who made it and how did they make it feel so real?

But JP never found out any of these things. When he got to the shops he was amazed to find that the shop had gone. Well, it was empty anyway. There was a board outside that read, *FOR SALE*.

JP went into the newspaper shop. "Excuse me, do you know where the junk shop next door has gone?" he asked the man in there.

The man gave him a funny look. "There's no junk shop next door," he said. "That place has been empty for weeks."

JP shook his head. How could that be true?

JP walked home. He was thinking hard. The whole thing was so weird – the junk shop, the man with the odd tuft of hair, the game that said it was for real … No, it was more than weird – it was creepy, scary.

JP looked at the game in his hand and he shivered. He wanted to get rid of this game, but he didn't want anyone else to have it. He mustn't put others in danger. He must put it somewhere where it couldn't do any harm, or make others risk their lives as he had done … He knew the perfect place.

He walked down to the river and onto the narrow, stone bridge that crossed it. He took one last look at the odd, deadly game in his hand. Then he threw it into the river. It plopped into the water with a small splash and was gone. JP stood for a moment or two, gazing down. Then he ran home for tea.

JP didn't play his GameBoy that night. He read a book. It was an old book his mum had got for him at a car boot sale. It had a rubbish cover, but the story was good. It was really exciting.

But not too exciting.

Our books are tested
for children and young people by
children and young people.

Thanks to everyone who consulted on
a manuscript for their time and effort in
helping us to make our books better
for our readers.

More *4u2read* titles...

How Brave Is That?
ANNE FINE

Tom's a brave lad. All he's ever wanted to do is work hard at school, pass his exams and join the army. He never gives up, even when terrible triplets turn his life upside down at home. But when disaster strikes on exam day, Tom has to come up with a plan. Fast. And it will be the bravest thing he has ever done!

Wartman
MICHAEL MORPURGO

Dilly has a wart called George and it's causing him a lot of grief at home and at school. Everyone calls him 'Wartman'. Can Dilly get rid of George and get his life back on track?

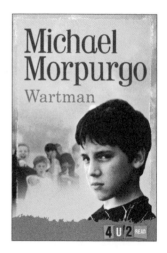

Mad Iris
JEREMY STRONG

Ross has a new pet – Mad Iris the ostrich! And she's got loose in the school!

Things are about to get really crazy...

Hostage
MALORIE BLACKMAN

"I'll make sure your dad never sees you again!"

Blindfolded. Alone. Angela has no idea where she is or what will happen next. The only thing she knows is she's been kidnapped. Is she brave enough to escape?

www.barringtonstoke.co.uk